ILLUMINATION PRESENTS

MINIONS

READER COLLECTION

LITTLE, BROWN AND COMPANY

New York Boston

Despicable Me 3: The Good, the Bad, and the Yellow
originally published in 2017 by Little, Brown and Company

Minions: Who's the Boss? originally
published in 2015 by Little, Brown and Company

Despicable Me: My Dad the Super Villain originally
published in 2010 by Little, Brown and Company

Despicable Me 2: Meet the Minions originally published
in 2013 by Little, Brown and Company

Despicable Me 3: Best Boss Ever originally
published in 2017 by Little, Brown and Company

Little, Brown and Company
Hachette Book Group
1290 Avenue of the Americas, New York, NY 10104
Visit us at LBYR.com

First Bindup Edition: June 2020

Little, Brown and Company is a division of Hachette Book, Inc.
The Little, Brown name and logo are trademarks of Hachette Book Group, Inc.

The publisher is not responsible for websites (or their content)
that are not owned by the publisher.

ISBNs: 978-0-316-42585-8 (pbk.), 978-0-316-53809-1 (paper over board)

Printed in China

APS

10 9 8 7 6 5 4 3 2 1

WELCOME TO
PASSPORT TO READING

A beginning reader's ticket to a brand-new world!

Every book in this program is designed to build read-along and read-alone skills, level by level, through engaging and enriching stories. As the reader turns each page, he or she will become more confident with new vocabulary, sight words, and comprehension.

These PASSPORT TO READING levels will help you choose the perfect book for every reader.

READING TOGETHER
Read short words in simple sentence structures together to begin a reader's journey.

READING OUT LOUD
Encourage developing readers to sound out words in more complex stories with simple vocabulary.

READING INDEPENDENTLY
Newly independent readers gain confidence reading more complex sentences with higher word counts.

READY TO READ MORE
Readers prepare for chapter books with fewer illustrations and longer paragraphs.

This book features sight words from the educator-supported Dolch Sight Words List. This encourages the reader to recognize commonly used vocabulary words, increasing reading speed and fluency.

For more information, please visit lbyr.com/passporttoreading.

Enjoy the journey!

Contents

The Good, the Bad, and the Yellow

Adapted by Trey King

Based on the Motion Picture Screenplay by
Cinco Paul and Ken Daurio

Attention, Minions fans!
Look for these words when you read this book. Can you spot them all?

bananas

vampire

unicorn

sidekick

MINIONS

Meet the **Minions**.
They are yellow, love bananas,
and work for super villains.

For years, the Minions searched for
the right villain to be their master.
They served a dinosaur, a caveman,

a pharaoh, and even a vampire.

But then they found Gru!

GRU

Gru was one of the greatest
super villains ever...
until he met three orphans.

They helped Gru learn that
happiness is more important.
Gru turned from “super bad”
to “super dad”!

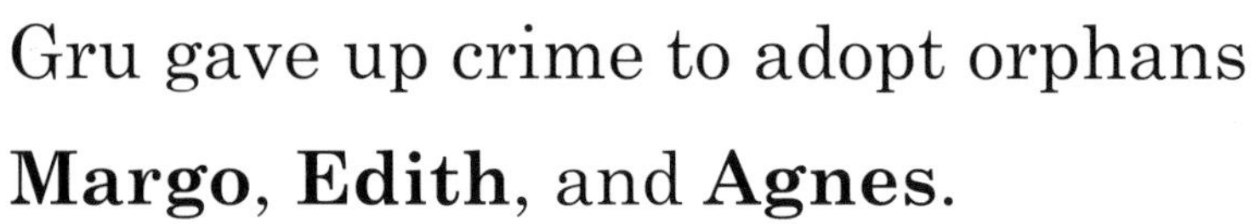

Gru gave up crime to adopt orphans **Margo**, **Edith**, and **Agnes**.

Then, Gru met **Lucy** and
joined the Anti-Villain League.
Lucy became his super-spy
partner and wife.
Together, they keep the world
safe from evil.

VALERIE DA VINCI

She is the new boss
of the Anti-Villain League.
And she is NOT nice.

After Gru and Lucy make a mistake,
Valerie fires them.
Then she throws them out of the blimp!

LUCY

Lucy is one of the world's best secret agents.
At least she was...until she lost her job.

If Lucy cannot be a perfect spy,
she can still be a perfect mother.
Lucy has three girls to keep out of trouble.

THE GIRLS

The girls lived in an orphanage
before they met Gru.
He needed to steal a shrink ray,
and they needed to sell cookies.
It turns out, they only needed
one another.

MARGO

Margo is the oldest
of the girls.
It is hard for her
to trust people.
But she loves her sisters.

EDITH

Edith is the middle daughter
and often up to no good.
She loves a good prank and is
always ready to hatch a scheme.

AGNES

The youngest of the girls,
Agnes thinks of others first.
She sells her favorite unicorn
to help pay the bills.

GRU'S MOM

Gru talks to his mom.

He asks if he has a brother.

Gru's mom tells the truth.
When Gru's parents split,
they each took a son.
She says she got second pick.

MEL AND THE MINIONS

Gru is no longer a secret agent
or an evil criminal.
Now the Minions are left without
any mayhem.
Mel has an idea....

The Minions go on strike!
But when they cannot find dinner,
pizza leads them to trouble.

DAVE AND JERRY

The other Minions left,
but Dave and Jerry stick around.
So Gru puts them in charge.

They join the family
on a trip to Freedonia.
Freedonia has lots of pigs
and Gru's brother!

DRU

Gru has a twin brother!

Gru and Dru look exactly the same—

except Dru has beautiful golden hair.

He lives in a huge house
with his butler, Fritz.
Pig farming is the family
business—or is it?

BALTHAZAR BRATT

Who is this guy?
He was an actor
on an old TV show.
His show was canceled,
but now he is back!

Clive is Bratt's robot sidekick.
He plays the best '80s music.
Bratt wants to become the villain
he played on TV.
He wants to get revenge....

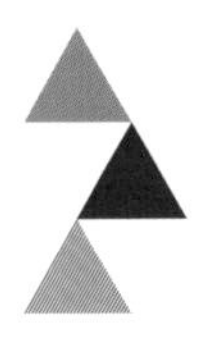

Bratt wants revenge on Hollywood.
Will Gru be able to stop him?
Who will win?

Only the Minions
know—for now.
Just wait and see!

Who’s the Boss?

by Lucy Rosen

Based on the Motion Picture Screenplay

Written by Brian Lynch

Attention, Minions fans!
Look for these words when you read this book. Can you spot them all?

yellow

caveman

dust

soldiers

See these funny yellow creatures?
They are called Minions.
Minions are small and round.
They go by many names,
like Dave, Paul, Carl, and Mike.

Each Minion is different,
but they all share the same goal:
to serve the most despicable master
they can find.

Minions have wandered the earth
for millions of years,
searching for the perfect villain
to be their master.

Masters were not hard to find,
but they were hard to keep.
Something always went wrong.

First there was the T. rex.
The Minions followed
the mighty beast as he stomped
through the forest.
They scratched his back.
They scrubbed his head.

They sent him flying
into a volcano by mistake.
“Whoops!” said the Minions.

Next came the caveman.
The Minions helped him
fight off wild animals.

Well, most of the time.

Minions have served some of the greatest leaders in history. Or they have tried to, at least.

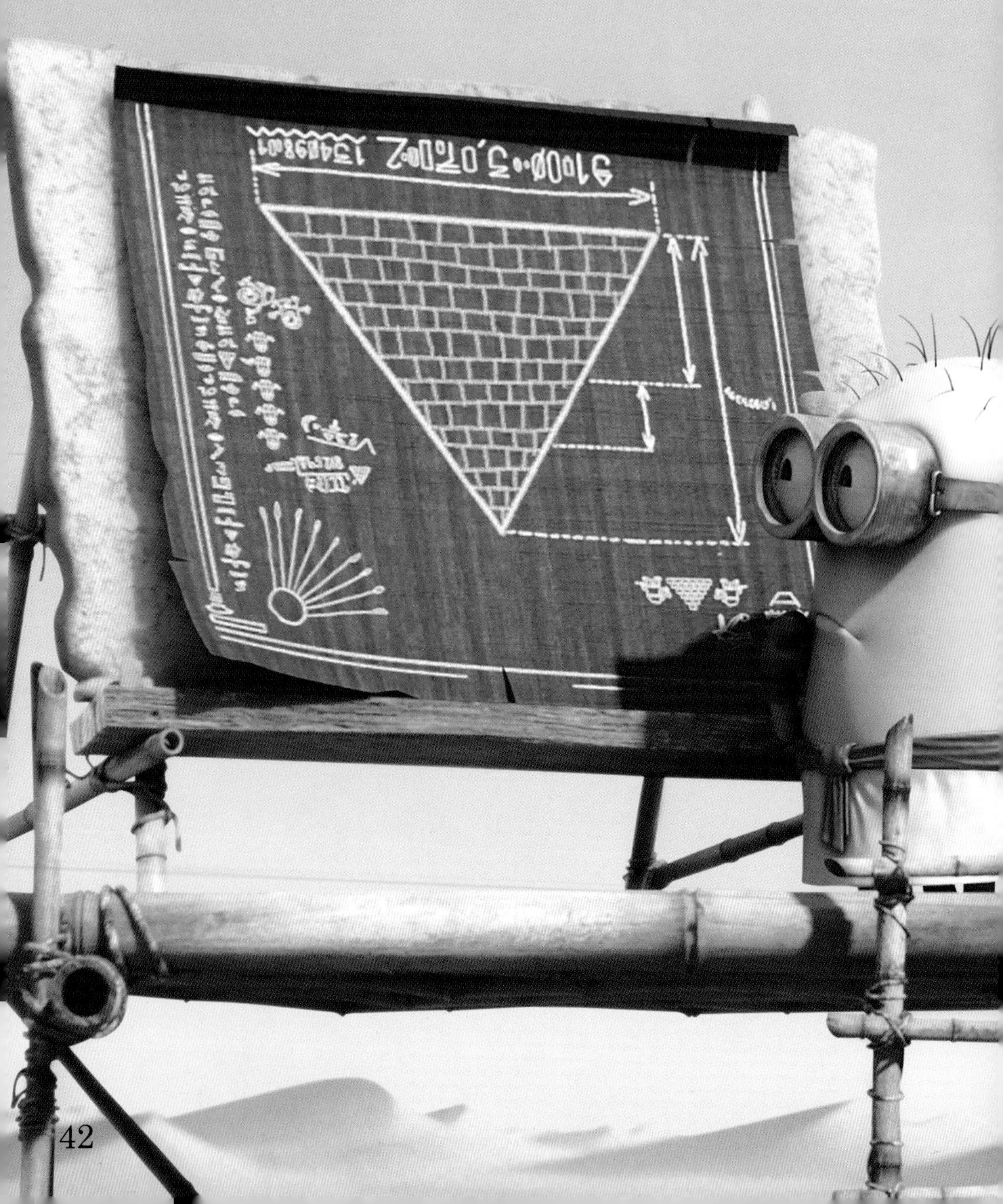

They built the pyramids in Egypt,
but they built them upside down.
This caused the pyramids to fall...
right on top of the pharaoh.

Then the Minions made Dracula their master, until they accidentally turned him into dust.

The Minions moved
from one evil villain to another.
They never seemed to find
their perfect fit.

Once, they stood by one of the world's fiercest and shortest generals.
It turned out that Minions
do not make very good soldiers.

The Minions did not give up hope,
no matter how often they failed.
And they failed a lot.

Finally, after being chased away
by the little general's army,
the Minions built a new home.
It was big enough for the whole tribe.

The Minions were safe.
They were secure.
They had everything
they could need.

But still, something was not right.
Without a bad guy to serve,
they had no purpose.

They became sad and aimless.
The Minions did not know
what to do.

But all was not lost,
for one Minion had a plan.
His name was Kevin.

Kevin would leave the cave
and not return until he found
his tribe the biggest, baddest
villain to serve!
But he needed help.
“Buddies,” said Kevin.
“Kiday come me!”

"Me coming!" said Bob,
the littlest Minion.
He was ready to help.
From the back of the room,
another hand went up.

Stuart had been volunteered by his friends while he was napping. And so the three Minion heroes got ready for their journey.

Kevin felt pride.

He would be the one to save his tribe.

Stuart felt hungry.

He would be the one to eat this banana.

And Bob?

Bob was scared of the journey ahead.
But as long as they stuck together,
Bob knew everything would be okay.

"Let us go!" cried the
three Minion friends.
It was time to find
a new despicable master!

My Dad the Super Villain

Adapted by Lucy Rosen
Based on the Story by Sergio Pablos
Based on the Screenplay by Cinco Paul and Ken Daurio
Illustrated by Rudy Obrero, Charlie Grosvenor,
Peter Moehrle, Dave Williams, and Keith Wong

Sleepy Kittens

Attention, Minions fans!
Look for these words when you read
this book. Can you spot them all?

Minion

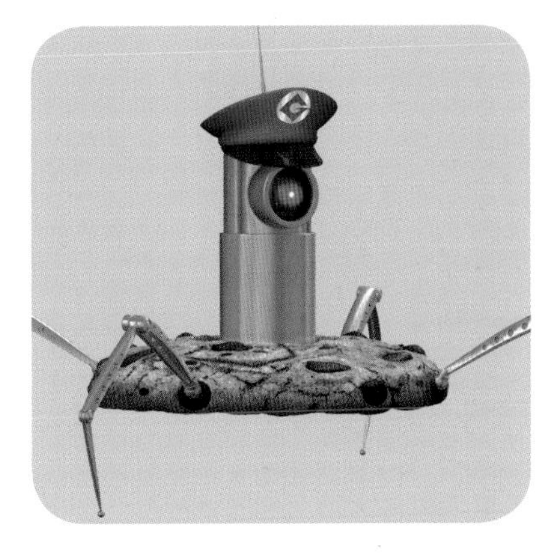

robot

Shrink Ray

ticket

Gru wanted to be the world's
number-one bad guy.
He lived in a big black house where
he hatched big, despicable plans.

Gru's latest plan was his
biggest idea yet.
"Assemble the Minions!" he called
as he entered his underground lab.

"Minions, we had a pretty good year
causing crime around the globe,"
Gru told his little workers.
"But next, we are going to do
something even bigger. . . .
We are going to steal the moon!"

There was only one problem.
Gru needed a Shrink Ray to make
the moon small enough to steal.
The only Shrink Ray around
belonged to Gru's nemesis, Vector.

Vector had alarms and
booby traps all over his house.
No one could break in.

Then Gru saw three little
girls outside Vector's house.
They were selling cookies for
the orphanage where they lived.
That gave Gru an idea.

Gru would adopt the girls!
The girls could deliver
boxes filled with Cookie Robots
to help Gru get inside Vector's
house and steal the Shrink Ray.

The girls were named
Margo, Edith, and Agnes.
"Here are the rules," Gru said
when he brought them home.
"You may not touch anything."

"Can we touch the floor?" said Margo.

"What about the air?" she asked.

This was going to be harder

than Gru had thought.

"Girls, let us go!" said Gru.
"Time to deliver the cookies!"
"Okay, but we are going
to dance class first," said Margo.
"We have a big show coming up."

Gru was annoyed.
He did not want to go
to dance class.

But Gru went anyway.

“Here you go,” said Agnes.

“It is a ticket to the dance show.

You are coming, right?”

“Of course, of course,” said Gru, rolling his eyes.

“Pinkie promise?” said Agnes.

Gru sighed.

“Oh, yes, my pinkie promises.”

After dance class, it was time to get the Shrink Ray from Vector's house. The girls delivered the cookies.

They did not know that Gru had hidden his Cookie Robots inside the cookie boxes.

The Cookie Robots helped Gru
by stealing the Shrink Ray
and handing it off to the minions.
Gru's plan worked perfectly!

Now that Gru had the Shrink Ray,
he was ready to be a full-time
villain again.
But he could not help spending
time with the girls.

Margo, Edith, and Agnes wanted
to go to Super Silly Fun Land,
so Gru went along for the ride.

The girls tried to win a
stuffed unicorn toy for Agnes,
and Gru lent a hand.

At bedtime, Gru
read the girls a book.
It was called *Sleepy Kittens*.

Before he knew it,
Gru was even having
tea parties with the girls!
The four of them were
becoming a family.

Still, Gru had not forgotten
about his big plan.
At last, he was ready
to steal the moon.

The moon was in the perfect position for stealing on the same night the girls had their dance show.

Gru could either make
his dream come true,
or he could be there
for his new family.

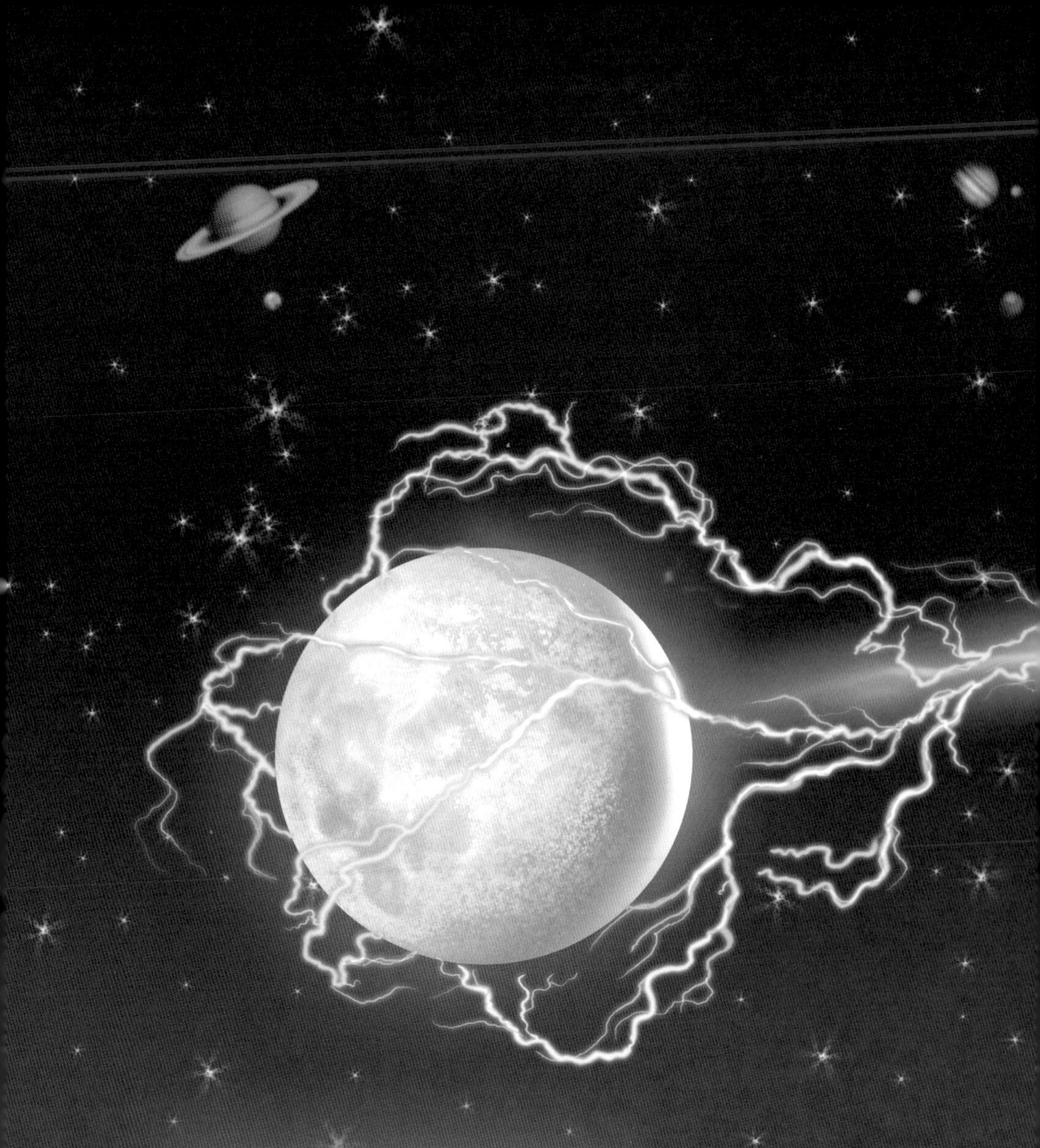

Gru made his choice.

He boarded his rocket ship.

He carefully aimed the Shrink Ray.

The moon got smaller and smaller.

But as Gru grabbed the moon
out of the sky, he suddenly
felt very alone.
His big moment had arrived,
but he had no one to share it with.

Gru remembered all the fun
he had shared with the girls.
And he remembered his
pinkie promise with Agnes.
He knew he had made a mistake.

“I can still make it!” Gru cried as he turned his ship around. He got there just in time.

Gru smiled as he took his
new family back home.
Who needs to be the world's
number-one bad guy when you can
be the world's number-one dad?

Meet the Minions

Adapted by Lucy Rosen
Based on the Motion Picture Screenplay
Written by Cinco Paul & Ken Daurio

TESTING IN PROGRESS

Attention, Minions fans!
Look for these words when you read this book. Can you spot them all?

fruit

jar

dragon

armor

Meet Dave and Kevin and Tom
and Stuart and Jerry.
They are all Minions.

They are just a few of the army of Minions who work in Gru's secret underground lab!

The Minions have one job,
and one job only:
They work for Gru.

The Minions love to
carry out his master plans.
Sometimes, they do not watch
out and can make a mess.

Once upon a time,
Gru was a super villain!
He even stole the moon
with the help of the Minions!

That was before Gru became
a dad to three girls.
Now, the Minions help him
raise Margo, Agnes, and Edith!
It can be just as hard!

The Minions help
with more than the girls.
They also help Gru
with his new business.

"My life of crime is over," says Gru.
"Now I am doing something sweeter.
Behold, my recipe for jams and jellies!"

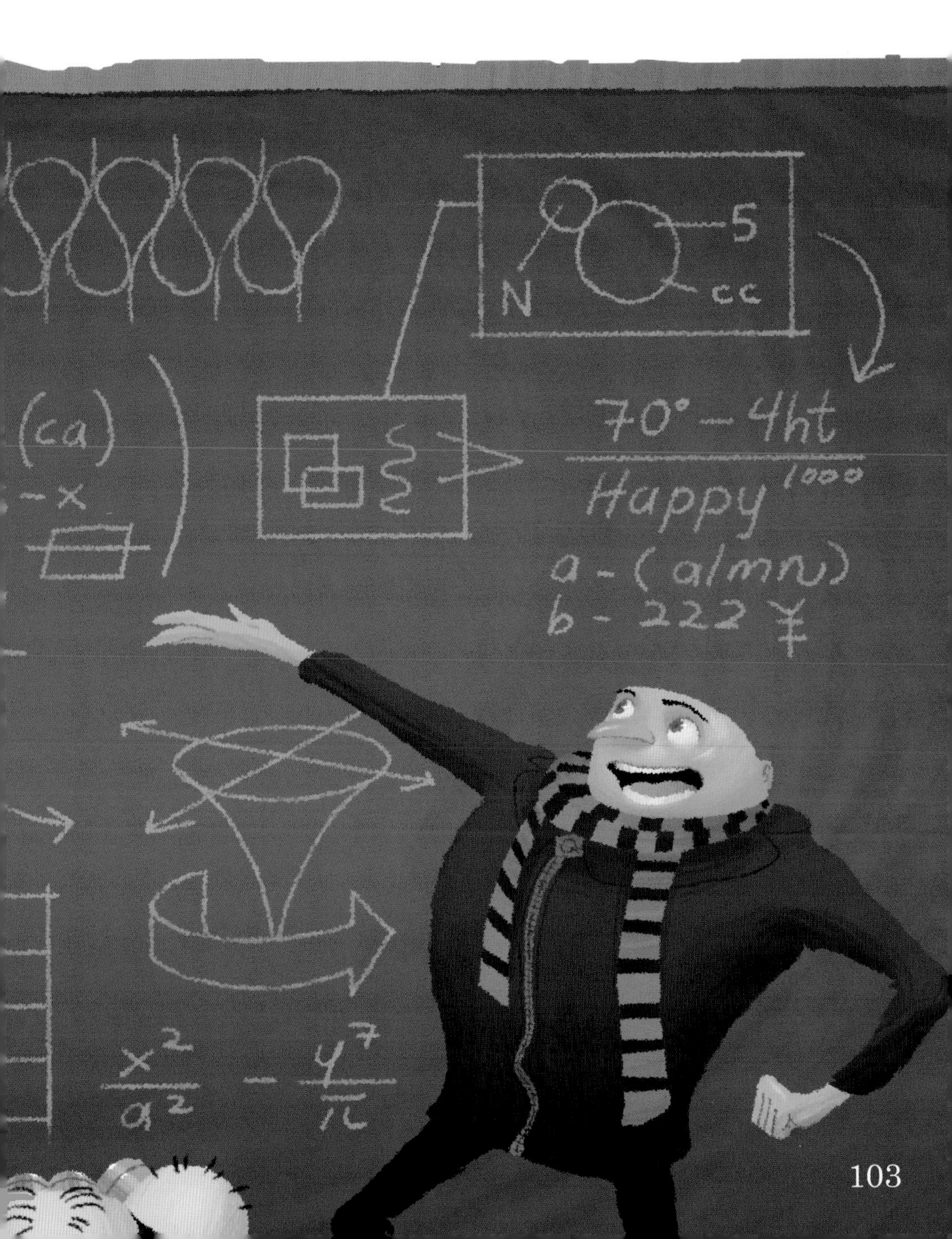

Dave puts up a sign that says
"Testing in Progress."
Some Minions start to mash fruit.
Others just make a mess.

At last, a jar is complete.
Gru calls the jam
Mr. Gru's Old-Fashioned Jelly!
The Minions cheer—until they taste it.
Yuck!

It may not be as exciting
as stealing the moon,
but Gru, the Minions, and the
girls seem pretty happy anyway.

When it is Agnes's birthday,
Gru throws her a princess party.
He invites her friends,
and they come in fun costumes.

"A dragon is coming!" says Agnes.
Kyle, their pet, is dressed up
as a dragon.

"Call the knights!" says Margo.
The Minions march out
wearing tiny suits of armor.
The Minions are the knights!

They pretend to attack Dragon Kyle.
They end up fighting one another.
Agnes laughs and tells them,
"Fight the dragon, not one another!"

The next day, something
strange happens.
A mysterious car
appears on the street.

Gru leaves the house
to check it out.
In a fiery flash, he is gone!
Someone has taken him!

Tom and Stuart peek around the corner just in time to see Gru disappear.

"Boss! Boss!" they shout as the car drives away.

Tom and Stuart look at each other. They know they have to act fast. Gru is in trouble, and the Minions have to help.

Tom leaps and lands on the car!
Stuart tries to jump, too,
but his suspenders get stuck.
He is pulled along.

The woman driving the car
is a secret agent named Lucy.
She spots the Minions
and captures them, too!
She zaps them with an
AVL-issued Lipstick!

Lucy takes Gru and the Minions
to the headquarters of
the Anti-Villain League.
"Gru, we need your help," says Lucy,
"to save the world from a super villain."

Gru thinks about the job offer.
He knows his jelly tastes gross,
so he and the Minions say yes!
It will be more fun to be super spies!

Back at home, Gru, Tom,
and Stuart tell the
other Minions about
their new mission.
All the Minions cheer!

The Minions never liked
the yucky jelly anyway.
They happily smash
all the jelly jars.

Gru is happier than ever.
He has a loving family,
an awesome new job,
and many Minions!

Best Boss Ever

Adapted by Trey King

Based on the Motion Picture Screenplay by
Cinco Paul and Ken Daurio

Attention, Minions fans!
Look for these words when you read this book. Can you spot them all?

T. rex

pyramid

shark

pigs

Minions have walked the earth
for millions of years.
They are looking for the perfect master.

Once, the Minions called a T. rex
their master.
But he fell into a volcano by mistake.

Oops!

The Minions' next master was a caveman. They helped him hunt wild animals—until a wild animal hunted him.

The Minions helped build the pyramids in Egypt.
But they read the plans upside down.
A pyramid fell on their new master.

Their next boss was the famous vampire, Dracula.

They opened the window
to let some sunlight in.
That was a bad idea.

The Minions have had lots of masters. None of them ever stuck around for very long.

There was always a shark or a cannon or something that got in the way.

Then they met Scarlet Overkill. They thought they had found their best master ever.

But she turned out to be a little too mean.

Finally, they met Gru.
They worked in the secret
lab under his house.

Gru was a despicable villain.
He had big plans to steal the moon!
It would be the biggest heist in all history!

The Minions love trouble.
They helped Gru steal a shrink ray.
(He needed it to shrink the moon.)

But another villain, Vector,
stole the shrink ray from Gru.
Gru and the Minions needed
to get it back.

That is how Gru and the Minions met three orphaned girls named Margo, Edith, and Agnes.

Gru and the Minions got the shrink ray back and stole the moon.

But Gru traded it all to become a father.

The Minions helped take care of the girls.
They made breakfasts—and messes.
They tucked the girls in at night.

They also helped Gru with his business,
making jams and jellies.
The Minions made a mess there, too.

When Gru met Lucy,
he became a super spy.
He was too busy being in love
to notice someone was taking
his Minions.

El Macho changed the Minions
into purple monsters.

Gru went after the evil Minions.
He had to save them.
But how?
His homemade jelly
may have tasted gross,
but it changed the Minions
back to normal.

Now the Minions are tired
of being heroes.
They miss being villains.
Mel leads them on strike!

Well, except for Jerry and Dave.

Jerry and Dave get to play
with pigs in Freedonia.

Meanwhile, Mel and
the Minions get hungry.
After they take some pizza,
they end up in jail.

Jail is terrible.
Mel and the other Minions
miss Gru.

Gru was the best boss ever!
Once they get out of jail,
they are going to make things right.

CHECKPOINTS IN THIS BOOK

The Good, the Bad, and the Yellow

WORD COUNT	GUIDED READING LEVEL	NUMBER OF DOLCH SIGHT WORDS
517	K	81

Who's the Boss?

WORD COUNT	GUIDED READING LEVEL	NUMBER OF DOLCH SIGHT WORDS
464	K	87

My Dad the Super Villain

WORD COUNT	GUIDED READING LEVEL	NUMBER OF DOLCH SIGHT WORDS
623	L	96

Meet the Minions

WORD COUNT	GUIDED READING LEVEL	NUMBER OF DOLCH SIGHT WORDS
521	L	87

Best Boss Ever

WORD COUNT	GUIDED READING LEVEL	NUMBER OF DOLCH SIGHT WORDS
436	K	74